Sky Royale: A Flight of Desire and Dissonance

Frank Spreader

Published by Frank Spreader, 2024.

This is a work of fiction. Similarities to real people, places, or events are entirely coincidental.

SKY ROYALE: A FLIGHT OF DESIRE AND DISSONANCE

First edition. December 15, 2024.

ISBN: 979-8230321484

Written by Frank Spreader.

Table of Contents

To those who dream of soaring beyond their limits,

who find themselves in moments they never imagined—

this story is for you.

And to everyone who's ever been torn between admiration and self-worth,

may you always find the strength to stay true to yourself,

no matter how turbulent the journey.

With gratitude to those who remind us that the stars are within reach,

even from the ground.

"The higher you soar, the smaller you appear to those who cannot fly."

— Friedrich Nietzsche

1.

"Welcome aboard Sky Royale. Settle in and let our dedicated crew pamper you as you soar ever higher. Here, it's not just about the flight—it's about flying in pure luxury. Indulge in service so exceptional, it doesn't just reach for the stars—it brings them down to you, one by one, until you feel like you're on top of the world. Even the clouds seem to bow in reverence to this experience."

The soft voice of a woman drifted through the air, barely a whisper, like a fleeting echo from another world, while the sharp click of a flight attendant's heels resonated through the lounge. The sound lingered, thick with anticipation, as if the luxury she spoke of had already begun to envelop you, even before you'd fully stepped on board.

Tasya glided toward a small hangar nestled beside the boarding lounge, her heels clicking softly on the pavement as twilight unfurled in shades of purple and indigo above. The lounge door swung open, and a cool breeze followed the flight attendant as she stepped into the evening. The airport lights flickered to life, forming clusters of stars scattered across the darkening ground, their faint glow a quiet prelude to the grandeur that awaited just beyond. There, parked in stillness, a sleek private jet stood ready, its polished frame softly glowing in the fading sunlight. The large airline logo on its tail caught the light, almost as if it were watching her.

She took a deep breath, a quiet smile tugging at the corners of her lips. Her heart thrummed in her chest—nervous, excited, and touched with a hint of pride.

She had made it. She'd been chosen for Sky Royale, the exclusive program reserved for VIPs, officials, and those whose names lingered in the air like a signature scent. This wasn't just any flight—it was *the* flight, a golden ticket to indulgence that promised rewards in ways beyond measure. Tips from passengers on this route were legendary, a siren call to every flight attendant eager to cater to the powerful. The competition to secure a spot on Sky Royale was fierce. Each time the program was announced, the bulletin board would light up, and within minutes, sign-ups would flood in—hundreds of hands raised for a chance at something beyond just a job. Something extraordinary.

And she had made it. Inside, every detail was crafted to the highest standard—the food, the drinks, each cushion and fabric, all meticulously chosen to satisfy the most refined tastes. Even the uniforms. A simple, elegant blue satin blouse paired with a short skirt. It was understated, yet in the most deliberate way, designed to be admired from afar—a quiet elegance that spoke volumes without saying a word.

"Just five minutes," the captain muttered, his eyes glancing at the face of his IWC Pilot's Mark XVIII.

"Only five minutes," the co-captain nodded, his gaze distant, as if he were already somewhere else, waiting for something just around the corner.

The flight attendant's fingers fumbled for a moment before she straightened the name tag on her chest. *Anastasia*—it gleamed under the harsh hangar light, almost too bright, as if daring anyone to look closer.

Tasya tugged at the satin blouse, smoothing it over her chest, then adjusted the short skirt, trying to get it to sit just right. But the fabric clung to her in ways that felt... off. The skirt, perhaps a little too short, rode higher than it should have, while the blouse tightened across her curves, drawing attention to things she'd rather not dwell on. The uniform had been tailored to her measurements by the company's seamstress, crafted with meticulous care. Yet now, there was something about it—something too tight, too revealing. But it didn't matter. Not really. It would have to do.

She didn't give it much thought. It wasn't worth worrying over, not now. She had learned long ago to set aside the small discomforts, letting them slip away like water off glass.

"You ready, Tay?" the captain asked, his eyes flicking down to the screen of his phone as he read the latest flight update. He didn't look up, but his voice carried a hint of something—maybe curiosity, maybe something more. "Is this your first SR flight?"

"Ready. Yep, Captain." Tasya nodded, but the movement felt unsteady, as if she were trying to convince herself more than him.

Her stomach twisted, tight and unrelenting, a knot she couldn't shake. The co-captain leaned in close, whispering something to the captain, his eyes flicking toward Tasya as if he were sizing her up. Then, without warning, both of them erupted in laughter—low, knowing, as if they shared a joke she wasn't quite in on.

Tasya quickly ran her fingers through her hair, adjusting the bun and straightening her scarf, making sure everything was in place. But the two men—Jesus—they just kept laughing, nudging each other like a pair of schoolboys. What the hell was going on? Was there something wrong with her face? Something she hadn't noticed? Something off?

"Chill, Tay," the captain said, sliding his phone back into his shirt pocket with a casual flick of his wrist. He shot her a quick glance, his eyes lingering just a moment too long, before offering a half-smile. "You're lookin real good in that."

"Thanks, Captain," Tasya muttered, her voice tight, as if she were trying to swallow something that wouldn't quite go down.

"You've got to give our customers the best service, you hear me? SR's our flagship, the crown jewel. It's the face of the whole damn airline. You can't let em down, not even a little. Personal service? That's the heart and soul of SR. You get that, right?"

Tasya took a deep breath, the air heavy in her lungs. This wasn't just any flight—it was her first Sky Royale, and the expectations... hell, they were off the charts. First-class service? That was nothing. Here, it was something else entirely, a whole new level of perfection she wasn't sure she could meet. The co-captain's eyes narrowed, a hint of something too knowing.

"You read up on everything for this flight?" he asked, his voice steady but carrying an edge—like he was waiting for something, or maybe testing her.

"Yeah, I've read it, Captain." Tasya nodded quickly, the words tumbling out a little too fast, as if she were trying to convince herself as much as them that she was ready for Sky Royale.

Ready for whatever it threw her way. How could she not be?

Tasya had come this far, hadn't she? For the past three days, she'd poured over the eighteen-hour itinerary for the flight from New York to Bangkok, memorizing every detail as if her life depended on it. Her job was to know everything—every passenger's quirks, their likes and dislikes, allergies, the exact moments she needed to step in for routine services. Everything had been mapped out by the reservation team, double-checked by management, and handed off to the select few tied to this flight. But there was one thing, one crucial thing, she still didn't know. And it gnawed at her.

"So, who's our passenger, Captain?" she asked, a flicker of curiosity in her voice. She had to know who this VIP was—the one she'd be catering to tonight. "An official, maybe? Or... someone else?"

"Tay, c'mon now," the captain interrupted, smiling as he wagged his index finger. "First rule of SR—privacy and anonymity. You don't breathe a word about the VIP flying with us tonight. Not a single syllable. Got it?"

Tasya fell silent, her lips pressed tight before she muttered, just loud enough, "Got it, Captain."

"He should be here by now, shouldn't he?"

"Shouldn't the passenger be in the lounge, like, fifteen or thirty minutes before the flight, Captain?" Tasya asked, glancing at her watch, a twinge of unease creeping up her spine. "Why the hell isn't this on schedule?"

"Maybe because they're a VIP," the captain said with a shrug, his tone almost lazy, as if it didn't matter. "Late or on time, that's their problem, not ours."

It didn't take long for them to spot what they were waiting for. A flash of white light sliced through the darkness outside the fence, sharp and blinding. An Audi glided down the narrow road near the lounge, its headlights cutting through the night, heading straight for the hangar where they stood, watching.

Tasya cleared her throat, a nervous flutter in her chest, as she adjusted her uniform for the hundredth time, making sure everything was perfect. Her heart began to pound, that familiar mix of excitement and dread creeping in as the realization hit—her first Sky Royale flight's VIP passenger had finally arrived.

She couldn't afford to mess this up. Her first impression would set the tone for the next eighteen hours in the air, and she knew all too well how quickly things could spiral if she slipped up.

Whoever was stepping out of that car, she knew she had to make the best impression—professional, friendly, with no room for hesitation. The car rolled to a slow stop beside the open airplane door, the makeshift stairs leading up to the cabin. The captain moved toward it, nodding at the driver in a silent command to open the door. As the Audi door creaked open, Tasya's smile clicked into place—sweet, practiced. Her hand instinctively cupped her chest as she gave a small, almost too-perfect bow.

"Welcome to Sky Royale!" she said, her voice smooth and warm, though tinged with an eagerness she couldn't quite mask. "Treat yourself to the best personal experience, above all else," she continued, the words slipping out almost automatically, the Sky Royale tagline she'd rehearsed so many times it had become second nature.

Her eyes widened, her breath catching in her throat, as the figure stepped out of the car. The tagline died on her lips, forgotten, as she stood frozen, staring at the VIP now standing right in front of her. The captain, sensing her shock, swiftly stepped forward, extending his hand to bridge the silence.

"Hey, welcome aboard! You ready to take off?"

2.

"Here's your welcome snack, sir," she murmured, her voice soft and tentative, as though the words might vanish into the air before reaching him.

"Thanks," the man muttered, his eyes briefly meeting Tasya's, lingering on her face as if trying to etch it into memory. "Anastasia, huh?" he said, the name slipping from his lips with a hint of uncertainty, as though it didn't quite belong.

"Anytime," Tasya replied, her smile warm but shadowed by a fleeting flicker in her eyes. "You can just call me Tasya, sir," she added, her voice velvety smooth, carrying the faintest hint of a warning beneath its charm.

"Alright, thanks. Tasya," the man repeated, drawing out her name as if savoring it, testing its taste on his tongue.

Tasya began to explain the buttons around the passenger's armrest, her fingers tracing each one with meticulous precision, as though she were guiding him through a map to a place he'd rather not visit.

"It's all good, Tasya," Donni interrupted, his tone casual, yet carrying an edge that made her hesitate. "I know my way around the buttons. Go ahead and take a break. It's a long flight, huh?"

"Alright then, I'll step out," Tasya murmured, straightening a few magazines on the table, her hands moving almost automatically before she turned and headed toward the crew room behind the cockpit. As she passed, she caught her reflection in the mirror. In that instant, as if a dam had burst, she couldn't help herself—her grin spread wide, so wide it felt like it might tear her face in half. She couldn't believe it.

Not yet. But damn, it was real. Her inner fangirl—screaming, wild, desperate to break free—was clawing at the walls of her mind. The VIP passenger she'd be tending to for the next eighteen hours, bound for Bangkok, wasn't just anyone. It was Donni Firman.

"Oh my God," Tasya whispered, her voice trembling with disbelief as she cupped her cheeks, excitement bubbling up inside her like a pressure on the verge of bursting.

Donni Firman. The lead singer of The Resonators. The band whose songs had been the soundtrack to her life since middle school—ten long years ago. Their easy-listening, heartfelt love ballads never sank into the cloying sweetness of other bands. The Resonators were an anthem for every girl her age, their romantic lyrics etching deep grooves into the hearts of young dreamers. And then there was Donni himself. The man who had stolen their breath away. The one who graced the stage shirtless, his athletic frame a living embodiment of the music, his voice casting a spell over the audience. Tasya and her friends would scream, hearts racing, drawn into his magnetic orbit as if he were a god, and they, his devoted worshippers.

Tasya had grown up in a modest family, where every penny counted. Yet there was one sacrifice she made without hesitation—she spent an entire month's worth of pocket money just to stream The Resonators' albums.

She didn't hesitate for a second. Her room, her diary—hell, even the corners of her mind—were plastered with posters and memorabilia, keepsakes of a band that, in some inexplicable way, had claimed a piece of her soul.

She'd spent her teenage years, her high school days, even the grueling hours of flight attendant training, with Donni's voice playing in the background—always there, a constant soundtrack to her life.

And now... now Donni was here. Right in front of her.

And now, here Tasya was, on a private jet with her idol. For a full eighteen hours. Assigned as his personal flight attendant, just for him. How the hell was she supposed to keep it together when her heart felt like it might tear itself apart? How could she resist the urge to pull out her phone, snap a picture, or post a story about spending this endless flight alone with him, the man she'd dreamed of for years?

"Oh my gosh!" She fanned her face, the heat of her skin a sharp contrast to the cool, artificial air of the cabin. "This is real, right? I'm not dreaming, am I?" Leaning back slightly, she peeked through the narrow gap in the cabin curtain, her breath caught in her throat.

There he was—Donni. Her idol. Sitting there, casually enjoying his cake as if it were the most ordinary thing in the world. But for Tasya, it was anything but ordinary. That was really him. The Donni Firman, the man who had lingered in the corners of her dreams for years, now sitting just a few feet away. It felt like some kind of trick, a moment suspended between the unreal and the impossible.

Donni Firman, now pushing forty, was somehow more captivating than ever. The handsome, chiseled face he'd worn in his younger years had deepened, with the subtle lines of age adding a mature allure and a quiet confidence that made him even more magnetic. His broad shoulders and well-muscled chest still had the power to make a twenty-three-year-old flight attendant's heart skip—hell, melt. Tasya's heart, already tight with the nerves of her first Sky Royale flight and the pressure of serving an unknown VIP, now hammered wildly in her chest. Because that VIP was Donni. The Donni.

Tasya nervously bit her lip, her thoughts spiraling in chaotic circles. *Am I even going to make it through this?* The question gnawed at her, relentless and sharp, like a warning she couldn't escape. It felt heavy, suffocating, as though it might crush her lungs. The microwave's chime cut through the fog of her fangirl daze, jolting her back to reality.

She snapped back to reality, her hands moving quickly as she plated the hot fettuccine, the appetizer for her idol. Standing before the mirror, Tasya adjusted her satin uniform, ensuring every crease was perfect, every line just right. A surge of confidence washed over her as the outfit hugged her curves in all the right places. The regular trips to the gym, the hours spent in yoga—they all felt worth it now, especially if Donni was the one taking notice.

She carefully arranged the meal on the plate, then pulled back the crew room curtain. Stepping into the space between worlds, where the hum of the jet and the weight of her nerves collided, she moved with practiced precision. In a few swift motions, she served the dinner, each step deliberate, as though the act of presenting it was a performance, tailored perfectly to the vocalist's every preference.

"Tasya," Donni called, his voice cutting through the air just as she was about to retreat back to her station.

"Yeah, sir?" Tasya forced the words out, her breath catching as her name slipped from his lips in that deep, commanding voice. She fought to keep her composure, her pulse racing. "Is there anything else I can help you with?"

"Hey, can you stay here with me?" Donni asked, gesturing casually toward the seat beside him. "You're not too busy, are you?"

"Definitely," Tasya replied, a smile tugging at her lips. She knew she had to deliver top-notch service on this Sky Royale flight, even for requests as simple as this. She sat down carefully, crossing her legs just enough to keep her skirt from riding up, the fabric clinging to her like a constant reminder of the delicate balance she had to maintain. Yet she kept her professionalism intact, holding onto it like a lifeline.

Even with Donni, a man whose fame spanned across the airwaves, he carried himself like someone you could talk to without fear. There was no trace of arrogance, no hint that his status was something to be worshipped or feared. His deep voice held her captive, and his intense gaze never faltered, locking onto hers as they spoke, as if he were trying to draw something out of her—something only he could see.

More than once, Tasya caught the weight of Donni's gaze sweeping over her from head to toe, an attention that twisted her insides—part fluster, part strange thrill. It was the kind of look that made her feel both exposed and invincible at once. As the minutes stretched into hours, the conversation shifted, and slowly, inevitably, it began to circle back to her. The words slipped out almost unintentionally—how she was a huge fan of The Resonators, and of course, Donni, the heart and soul of the band. They hung between them, raw and honest, like a confession she hadn't meant to make.

"Thanks, man." Donni leaned back in his seat, folding his arms across his chest, a subtle smile tugging at the corners of his mouth. "Didn't expect to run into a fan like you—especially one who's gotta take me all the way to Bangkok."

"For me, it's an even bigger surprise," Tasya admitted, her hand instinctively pressing over her heart, the sincerity of her words settling heavily between them. "It's truly an honor to have you as my first SR passenger, Mr. Firman."

"Nah, Tasya," Donni countered, his voice low and smooth, like he was sharing a secret. "For the last ten years, you've been all in on my music—what more could a guy like me ask for? Seriously, it's an honor for me. Especially to have a fan who's..." He paused, his eyes sweeping over her with a casual gesture of his hand. "...as beautiful as you are."

His words lingered in the air, heavy with intent, as if they were more than just a compliment—more than he'd meant to say. Oh, wow. The way he phrased it sent a rush of heat to Tasya's face, as though she'd been touched by something invisible and electric.

Tasya was sure her cheeks were as red as a boiled shrimp. She quickly lowered her head, desperate to shield her face—and the frantic thumping of her heart—from the praise of her idol. The moment hung in the air, suspended in time, as if this first Sky Royale flight was shaping up to be a memory she'd never forget, one burned deep into her.

3.

The jet engine droned with a low, steady hum, a restless ghost murmuring in its sleep. Nine hours had vanished into the night, the plane slicing through an endless sea of black, halfway to its destination. Below, the world lay still, cocooned in the cold embrace of slumber, blissfully unaware of the storm brewing above. Inside, the cabin pulsed with life—a rhythm of music that seeped into the bones and the bright, unrestrained laughter of a girl basking in the euphoria of meeting her idol. It was a sound that defied the stillness of the skies, an electric spark in the void.

.

Let me prove it to the world,
I'll show you where to go, unfurled.
With dreams that never fade or fall,
Watch me as I stand tall.

.

As the last notes of *Unstoppable Dreams* dissolved into the air, Tasya unleashed a wild, jubilant scream—a raw, unfiltered outburst of pure joy, the kind that only erupts when a lifelong dream becomes reality. There she was, seated beside her idol, the original voice behind the song, harmonizing to The Resonators' greatest hits. These were more than just melodies to her; they were the soundtrack of her life, a refuge through the darkest times. The lyrics spilled from her effortlessly, like a sacred language etched into her soul, her voice entwined with the music in a moment of rapturous devotion.

"Yo, Tasya," Donni said, his tone playful yet warm. "You've got one hell of a voice. I might need to watch my back—my spot as lead vocalist could be in serious danger." He laughed, the sound rich and genuine, clapping his hands as if embracing the challenge. "You've clearly got a solid handle on a lot of our songs, huh?"

"Absolutely, sir," Tasya replied, her voice firm, carrying a subtle edge that dared him to question her. She straightened, puffing out her chest in a quiet gesture of pride—a small move that felt larger than life, as if she were steeling herself against an invisible force only she could sense.

Especially coming from the lead vocalist of her favorite band—the man she'd spent years admiring from afar. It felt surreal, like stepping into a dream she never wanted to end.

"I'm your biggest fan, Mr. Firman," Tasya murmured, her voice scarcely more than a whisper, as though the words were sacred—something she'd cherished for years, waiting for the perfect moment to release them into the world.

Donni leaned back in his seat, a slow smile spreading across his face as he shook his head, a blend of disbelief and quiet admiration flickering in his eyes. His gaze lingered briefly on the flight attendant before shifting to the half-empty glass of whiskey in his hand. He swirled it thoughtfully, the ice clinking in a rhythm that seemed almost intentional, a subtle punctuation to his musings. "Getting this SR package was definitely a smart move," he said, his voice smooth and unhurried, the words carrying the weight of a practiced ritual. He lifted the glass, savoring a measured sip. "The flight attendant with me? She knows exactly how to make this flight unforgettable. Service is flawless."

Tasya beamed, her smile stretching wide, lighting up her entire face. "I'm so happy too," she said, her voice bubbling with excitement. "You're my first SR passenger! This... this is really something special." She paused, her eyes shimmering with a joy that hinted she already knew this moment would stay with her forever.

"Nah, you're the one making this special, Tay," Donni said, pointing at her with deliberate emphasis, his tone heavier with meaning than usual. He set his whiskey glass down with a soft clink and leaned forward, his gaze locking onto hers, steady and unyielding. "And a moment like this?" He let the words linger, the weight of them settling between them. "It's not something you let pass by. How about we celebrate it, just a little?"

Tasya hesitated, the question hanging between them, as her mind worked its familiar quiet rhythm when faced with a choice. She recalled the crew storage room, hidden behind the usual clutter, where party supplies were kept for moments like this—spontaneous and unexpected. "What kind of celebration do you have in mind, Mr. Firman?" she asked, her voice smooth, like a subtle invitation. "I can set up games, drinks, whatever you'd like." She offered the words with a kind of eager confidence, the sort that comes from knowing she could make the moment unforgettable.

"Anything works?" Donni asked, his eyes narrowing as he fixed her with a steady, intent gaze.

"Yeah." Tasya nodded, her head tilting slightly, as if she were weighing the words before letting them fall.

It was the kind of nod that made you wonder what she was holding back, what words she wasn't letting slip. For some reason, Donni's gaze shifted, an unfamiliar weight settling in the pit of his stomach. It wasn't like before—there was something different now, as if the air had thickened, charged with an unspoken tension.

"What if I want you instead?" Donni said, the words slipping out slower than he intended, as if they'd been lurking in the dark corners of his mind, waiting for the right moment to step into the light.

The moment the words hit her ears, Tasya froze, her body stiffening in place. It wasn't the first time she'd heard a question like that, but it still felt like a cold draft sweeping through the room—unsettling, sharp, and carrying a warning she couldn't quite shake. Since starting her flight attendant training, she'd encountered questions like these more than once—always from someone who thought they could get away with it: colleagues, captains, or the occasional crude passenger.

She knew exactly what it meant—a silent invitation to something she had no interest in, something that had nothing to do with her job.

Without hesitation, she shut it down. She was a flight attendant, not an object. It wasn't just pride; it was the simple truth—she couldn't let a man, especially one she didn't love, touch her. No, it wasn't that easy. Not for her.

She wasn't a saint. She'd been intimate before, but it had never been with just anyone. No, she believed that sex wasn't something to be casually handed out, like a quick fix. To her, it had to be more than skin-deep. It needed to mean something—an emotional connection, real and lasting desire, not the mindless gratification that animals chase after.

She couldn't lower herself to that. Tasya had always reserved intimacy for someone who truly mattered—her boyfriend, and even then, it had only happened once or twice. She wasn't promiscuous, not even with someone she liked. But what if the person asking wasn't just anyone? What if it was someone she'd idolized for the last ten years? That was a different kind of temptation, a line she'd never imagined crossing.

"Uh, well..." She stammered, her words faltering as she struggled to make sense of what Donni meant.

The air grew thicker, each second stretching longer, heavier, as if his question were pressing down on her chest. In an instant, the lighthearted atmosphere they'd shared shifted, twisting into something uncomfortable, sharp—a silence that crawled between them, making the room feel cold and awkward.

"What do you mean, sir?" Tasya asked, her voice barely above a whisper, as if she feared the question itself might unravel something she wasn't ready to confront.

"I want to celebrate this incredible night with you, Tasya," Donni said, his voice low, almost intimate. He reached out, his hand moving slowly and deliberately to tuck a strand of her hair behind her ear.

The touch was casual, but there was something in it—a shift, a strange weight that hung in the air like a spark, ready to ignite. It was brief, but it left a lingering warmth on her skin. The heat from his fingers seemed to trail down her neck, making her flinch, her body reacting before her mind could catch up.

"For a musician like me," Donni said, his voice thick with reverence, "meeting a fan who's been vibing with my work for ten years? That's the highest form of appreciation." He leaned in slightly, his gaze locking onto hers. "Especially when that fan is someone like you."

Tasya looked down, her teeth sinking into her bottom lip as nerves twisted in her gut. She tried to push the unease aside, her fingers gripping the hem of her satin skirt, as if holding onto it could anchor her, preventing her from drifting away under the weight of the moment.

"I'm sure a lot of guys have told you how beautiful you are, right?"

Donni's voice was soft, almost coaxing, as his fingers brushed through her hair, tracing the curve of her neck and the base of her skull. It should've felt intrusive, but strangely, it didn't. The touch was slow, deliberate, as if he knew exactly how to navigate the line between familiar and unfamiliar.

For reasons she couldn't quite explain, Tasya didn't pull away. She sat there, her pulse quickening, as his touch lingered. "Yeah, sir," she replied, her voice shaky, the words slipping out more like a breath than an answer.

"To me, you're the very definition of beauty," Donni said, his voice low, almost reverent. "You're everything a woman should be."

The words hung in the air, thick and heavy, as if meant to burrow deep inside her, taking root in the hidden corners of her soul she hadn't even realized were exposed. It was no wonder he was the heart of The Resonators. His gift for weaving words, turning them into something both intimate and inevitable, was undeniable.

Tasya knew those words were just flattery—nothing more. Yet, they had a way of settling into her chest, making her heart race in spite of herself.

She glanced at Donni, his calm demeanor a sharp contrast to the turmoil brewing inside her.

Donni sat there, unruffled, while her pulse hammered in her ears, as though it might burst through her skin.

Tasya didn't know what to do. It was one of those moments where everything felt suspended, as if the world itself were holding its breath, waiting for her to make a choice.

But she was frozen, trapped in the grip of something she couldn't name.

"So, you want to spend the night with me?"

Tasya froze, her breath catching in her throat as her mind scrambled, a thousand thoughts colliding in a blur. What kind of question was that? It lingered in the air like a shadow—too heavy to ignore, too strange to make sense of.

Of course, she didn't want to—at least, she thought she didn't. But why couldn't she find the words? Why did it feel like her throat had tightened, her voice stolen away? The silence stretched on, thick and uncomfortable, tightening around her like a vise. It didn't take long for Donni to notice.

Donni cleared his throat, the sound cutting through the thick silence like a knife. Without looking, he reached for his whiskey glass, tilting it to drain the last sip with a smooth, almost careless motion. Rising to his feet, he adjusted his shirt, the fabric rustling softly. Slowly, he extended his hand toward Tasya, the gesture deliberate and unhurried. Leaning in just enough for his breath to stir the air between them, he whispered, his voice low, almost like a command, "Let's go."

He slid the lock into place, the soft click sealing the bedroom suite at the rear of the plane. It wasn't much—just a small, tidy room meant to make long flights bearable, even pleasant, for passengers desperate to stretch out. Yet, something about it felt almost suffocating. Tasya's gaze swept over every detail: the bed, perfectly made with crisp sheets and a thick silk blanket, looked inviting, but there was a dissonance beneath the surface. The polished wood gleamed in the dim light, everything arranged with almost obsessive precision, as if the cabin was trying too hard to be flawless. A small nightstand by the bed held a minibar, stocked with expensive drinks—too many choices for anyone seeking peace. The air was cool, perhaps too cool, and a faint, almost sickly-sweet scent lingered, drifting from somewhere unseen. It wasn't luxury. It was the unnerving perfection of something engineered to be flawless—and in the process, lost all sense of comfort.

"Take a seat," he said, his voice flat—more of a command than a suggestion.

Tasya lowered herself onto the edge of the bed, her shoulders slumped as if the weight of some unseen burden had settled deep inside her. Her gaze drifted to Donni's jeans, then to the polished shoes that stood just inches from her.

She couldn't bring herself to look up—not yet. Not with him so close.

She felt like a marionette with tangled strings, the kind of awkwardness that made her skin crawl. She couldn't summon the strength to lift her eyes—not to his face, not to the one person she'd admired from afar for so long. Was this really happening? Or was she dreaming?

Anastasia—the girl from nowhere—was locked in a bedroom with Donni Firman. And soon, she told herself, they would be together. *Doing it.* God, it felt like something pulled from a sick, twisted fantasy.

Donni slipped off his diver's watch and set it down on the minibar with quiet finality. "Appreciate it, Tasya."

His hand moved with a slow, deliberate tenderness, his fingers grazing her chin before tilting her face upward. Her wary, trapped eyes met his, unable to escape the quiet insistence of his touch. His fingers traced a path along her cheek, down to her jaw, then slid behind her ear—each movement soft, unsettling, and lingering just a moment too long.

"Really glad you're up for celebrating this with me," Donni said, his voice low and almost too warm, laced with an undercurrent of something unspoken.

His hand was broad and warm against her cheek, a sharp contrast to the chilled air circulating through the cabin. The warmth seeped into her skin, and before she realized it, her eyes fluttered shut, instinct taking over.

Tasya savored the warmth of Donni's hand on her face, each stroke sending her pulse racing—a tangled blend of tension, shyness, and an unsettling, unexpected comfort. Without realizing it, her lips began to part—a subtle, involuntary movement, like a red flower slowly blooming to reveal a glimmer of pearl-white teeth.

She was unfolding, inviting—like nectar luring a bee. Eyes still closed, she let herself sink deeper into his touch. Then, in that suspended moment, something soft, warm, and insistent met her lips.

"Mmh..."

A soft murmur escaped her lips as Tasya jerked back, surprise rippling through her. Her eyes snapped open, widening as she found a face mere inches from hers, close enough to blur the world around them. Donni's lips had barely brushed hers—a fleeting kiss—but it was enough to send her heart racing wildly, pounding as though it might burst free from her chest.

Donni flashed a slow, knowing smile as his hands drifted downward, his fingers brushing the delicate scarf tied around Tasya's hair. With a gentle tug, he unraveled it, letting the fabric slip free as her long, dark hair cascaded around her shoulders like silk, catching the dim light. He tossed the scarf carelessly onto the bed behind her, then stepped back, his eyes lingering on her, as if trying to take in every detail.

For a moment, Tasya was no longer just a flight attendant—she was something far more captivating, more real.

"You know, Tasya," Donni murmured as he moved closer, his fingers threading through her soft hair with deliberate precision, "the woman sitting right in front of me? She's exactly what every guy dreams of." His words were a weapon, carefully chosen to unravel her. Then, with a smooth, unhurried motion, he guided her back, gently pressing her onto the bed.

Tasya couldn't move, couldn't breathe, her chest tight with anticipation as she watched Donni crawl toward her, his eyes fixed on hers, his movements slow and deliberate.

Donni stopped just above her, a shadow casting over her. Oh my God. This wasn't a fantasy, a dream she could wake from. It was real.

Tasya was here—on her first Sky Royale flight, in the cabin, with Donni Firman. It had never even crossed her mind, not in a million years of being his devoted fan. Yet, here it was. This was happening. And it was real.

Donni hovered over her, silent, his gaze heavy and unwavering as it traced every inch of Tasya's flushed face. His eyes lingered on her tight satin blouse, watching how it clung to her breasts, rising and falling with her quickened breath.

He watched as the short skirt inched up, revealing the smooth, pale length of her thighs and a fleeting glimpse of her panties—each detail marking her, as if she were something he had all the time in the world to savor. Tasya's hands, trembling with unease, clung to the lower sides of Donni's shirt, desperate for something to steady herself, desperate for something to hold onto.

Then, without a sound, he moved his thumb—a slow, almost casual motion, as if he weren't even aware of it—gently brushing across her full, red lower lip. The touch was light, almost reverent, as if he were testing the softness of her skin, savoring it, as though it were the only thing in the world that mattered.

"You're stunning," he whispered, his voice low, as if the words had been pulled from somewhere deep inside him.

Tasya had no time to react before Donni closed the distance between them, his face drawing near with a quiet, inevitable certainty. In an instant, his lips pressed against her lower lip—soft and sudden, as if there was no turning back now.

"Mmmhh..." Tasya let out a soft moan, the sound barely escaping her—a quiet, involuntary gasp caught in her throat.

Donni's lips lingered for a moment before he gently sucked on her lower lip, nibbling just enough to send a shiver through her. His tongue skimmed across her lips, slow and deliberate, leaving a soft sweep that made them tingle.

Donni pulled back for a breath, then kissed her again, his lips slick with the moisture of their contact. Like a cat toying with a mouse, he teased her, his movements calculated, watching for any sign, any response to the silent challenge he had laid down.

Tasya closed her eyes, letting the darkness consume her. Her hand moved slowly, almost trembling, as it traced the smooth curve of his back, stopping just at his shoulders. Her breath became shallow, coming in sharp, quick bursts.

She could feel her mouth opening wider, as if something deep inside her had finally given way.

Donni smiled into the kiss, a small, knowing curve of his lips. He tilted his head, deepening the connection, then slid his tongue into her mouth—slow and deliberate, as if claiming his place.

"Ngghhh..."

Tasya's breath caught in her throat, the sound slipping from her lips, barely audible, as if it had been wrenched from her. Donni's tongue brushed against hers, slow and deliberate, a gentle sweep that sent a shiver through her. It felt rough, yet impossibly wet, leaving behind the lingering taste of sweet whiskey—thick and warm—on her tongue.

Tasya licked the last traces of sweetness from Donni's tongue, her senses consumed by the taste.

For a moment, Donni let her have it, giving her the space to take whatever she needed, to hold onto the sweetness as if it were something precious, something she could keep. He watched her, intrigued by her reaction—far more than he'd expected. Outside, the hum of the airplane's engines faded into silence. Inside the bedroom cabin, it was still—eerily still.

Tasya could hear the frantic rush of her own breath, the steady thrum of her heartbeat in her chest. She didn't pull away, continuing to kiss him, her lips clinging to his as if she couldn't bear to let go of the lingering taste of whiskey—sweet and intoxicating. The blood in her body surged, rushing through her veins, pooling in one aching, desperate point.

She felt a strange, pulsing heat deep within her, a sensation building in her lower body as if something were awakening there. Donni's hand moved slowly, almost deliberately, grazing the soft line of her hair, brushing the edge of her ear, and then down her neck. His fingers drifted lower, exploring the curves of her waist, each touch leaving a trail of warmth that seemed to seep through her blue satin blouse, as if his touch could burn right through the fabric.

And then, with a sudden jolt, she realized the hand was moving lower. And lower still. Tasya's eyes snapped open, and she broke the kiss, pulling back sharply.

She stared at Donni, her gaze fixed and wide, as if trying to make sense of what had just happened.

"Tasya, hey."

Tasya shoved at Donni, her hands pressing against him, desperate to create some space. Oh my God. What had just happened? Had she really just done that?

For a moment, she had lost herself—let go, allowing the moment to carry her away. She'd dropped her guard, followed him into that locked room without a second thought, and let him kiss and touch her. Even if it was Donni Firman. Was she really the kind of girl who would do something like that?

She felt like an utter fool. As Donni leaned in again, she quickly turned her face away, her heart racing. The confusion on his face deepened, only adding to the turmoil in her own mind.

"Yo, what's going on, Tasya? You change your mind or something?"

Tasya didn't answer. She kept pushing against Donni, her hands pressing against him, but he didn't budge. It was as if he were made of stone.

"Hey, uh, excuse me, sir."

"Yo, where you headed?" Donni asked, his grip firm as he cupped her cheek, gently turning her face toward him.

The softness on his face evaporated, replaced by a cold, blank stare. It made Tasya's courage wither, her gaze faltering under the weight of his emotionless expression.

"Wasn't tonight supposed to be about celebrating with me?" Donni asked, his voice flat, with a hint of something darker lurking beneath the words.

"But, like, sir, this is..." Tasya stammered, her throat tight as she swallowed hard.

"You forget, Tasya?" Donni leaned in close, his breath warm against her ear. "In Sky Royale, I get the VIP treatment. I can have whatever I want on this plane."

His large hand closed around Tasya's thigh, squeezing with a firmness that felt almost deliberate. The grip seemed to say he had her, that he was in control, and she was powerless to stop it. Tasya's breath caught as she felt Donni's hand move slowly, the light fabric of her satin skirt offering little barrier between them.

"And that includes you," Donni said, his voice low, almost a whisper, but carrying a weight that made her heart skip.

She froze, her body coiled tight with tension as Donni's hand slid inside, his touch igniting a wave of sickening unease that crawled under her skin. "Ugh..." A strained sound escaped her as she pushed against his hand, frantic to break free, but his grip held fast—unyielding, deliberate, a predator savoring its control.

Donni leaned in, his lips seeking hers, but Tasya pressed her mouth firmly shut, her jaw tight as steel—a silent, unyielding refusal carved into her expression.

Tasya wrenched her face away, straining to put distance between them, a desperate act of defiance that shattered the last vestiges of Donni's patience. His hand darted out, seizing a fistful of her long hair, and with a brutal yank, he dragged her head back toward him, his simmering frustration erupting into raw, cruel aggression.

Donni slammed his lips against Tasya's in a harsh, graceless act, stripped of tenderness or consent—a collision driven by something raw, dark, and unrestrained.

"Mmmph..."

Her muffled groan was smothered beneath the crushing weight of his lips, a sound silenced before it could fully form. This kiss bore no trace of the earlier hesitant softness; it was all jagged edges, all brute force, an empty, ravenous hunger. Her heartbeat seemed to vanish, swallowed by the stifling stillness that hung heavy in the air. Meanwhile, her skin, dry and chafing against Donni's fingers, began to ache—a sharp, grating discomfort that felt as if even her body rebelled against the intrusion.

Tasya clenched her eyes shut, willing the world to vanish around her. Donni's lips hovered over hers, pressing softly, lingering as he sank deeper into the kiss. He savored it, as though chasing a taste he couldn't quite capture, the faint sweetness of her warmth clinging to him, wrapping his senses in a dark, intoxicating haze.

She felt trapped in Donni's unyielding grip, the pull of her hair forcing her to endure the kiss—intense yet hollow, stripped of anything resembling the fantasies she'd once cherished. Her mind, as if seeking refuge, drifted back to those early years when she and her friends had screamed his name with breathless excitement, their collective admiration almost palpable, hanging in the air like a dream too vivid to forget.

She remembered the electric thrill of watching him on stage, his sweat glistening under the lights as he sang with unrestrained intensity—an untouchable idol, larger than life. Alone in her room at night, she had dreamed of being close to him, of feeling his strength and presence envelop her. But now, here she was, living the moment she had once fantasized about—serving him as a flight attendant, held in his arms. Yet this... this wasn't the dream she had imagined. A single tear slid quietly down her cheek, her soft sobs barely audible, lost in the oppressive silence around her.

After what felt like an eternity, Donni finally pulled away, his breath ragged. His eyes fell on Tasya's face—tears tracing down her cheeks, her expression a fragile blend of confusion and vulnerability. The sight of her, so striking yet so powerless, made him pause for the briefest moment, a flicker of something unreadable crossing his gaze before he swiftly pushed it aside.

"Why's that?" he asked, his voice low and deliberate, as his hand slid out from beneath her panties with an excruciating slowness, each movement measured, calculated. He released her hair, but his fingers lingered, brushing against the strands as if unwilling to let go. "You don't want this?"

Tasya stayed silent, her breath hitching as she wiped away her tears with the back of her trembling hand, each motion hurried, desperate to patch the cracks before they grew too wide. She kept her gaze fixed downward, unable to meet Donni's eyes—dreading not just what she might see in them, but the truths he might uncover in hers.

Donni's eyes lingered on her tear-streaked face, each fragile sob a silent echo of the turmoil gripping her. With a measured shift, he pulled back, easing his body away from hers and rolling onto the bed beside her. His chest rose and fell heavily, the space between them charged with an unspoken weight—something raw and unnamed, hanging in the air like an unfinished thought.

Donni dragged a hand over his forehead, his eyes clenched shut as though he could press away the weight pressing down on him. "Just... get out," he muttered, his voice flat and empty, stripped of emotion—like a man too drained to feel anything anymore.

"Excuse me, sir?" Tasya's voice trembled as she perched on the edge of the bed, her body rigid, every muscle tensed as though bracing for an inevitable blow she couldn't outrun.

"Just go back to your post," Donni said, his tone flat and detached, as he waved a dismissive hand, brushing Tasya off like an afterthought and motioning her out of the cabin.

But Tasya remained rooted in place, her feet unwilling to carry her away. The weight of guilt bore down on her, heavy and unrelenting, for denying the VIP's request. "I'm sorry, sir. I..." she began, her voice faltering under the strain.

"What are you still doing here?" Donni snapped, his voice cutting through the air like a blade, edged with rising frustration. "I told you to leave. Didn't I make myself clear?"

Tasya remained frozen beside him, her eyes glistening with fresh tears. Her shoulders trembled with each uneven breath, as she fought to suppress the sobs threatening to escape.

She felt like a complete failure—her first flight with Sky Royale already unraveling, each moment adding to a weight she couldn't shake.

"Are you mad at me, sir?" Tasya asked, her voice quivering beneath the steady stream of tears.

Seeing the tears still clinging to her cheeks, Donni sat up slowly, his movements cautious, almost reluctant. He reached out, his fingers brushing softly against her skin, wiping away the traces of sorrow with an unexpected tenderness. "Nah, Tay, you got it wrong," he murmured, his voice low and intimate, like a secret whispered in the dark. "I'm not askin you to leave cause I'm mad at you. I'm askin you to leave cause... I know I won't be able to stop myself if you stay. You saw what just went down, right? I pushed you too far... made you cry."

Tasya lifted her gaze to Donni, her eyes shimmering with unshed tears, raw and vulnerable, as if they carried a weight too heavy to speak.

"I can't stand seein you cry like this," Donni murmured, a faint smile tugging at his lips, his gaze softening as it lingered on her tear-filled eyes. "You're too damn beautiful to be cryin, Tasya."

Tasya sat frozen, his words echoing in her mind, replaying on a loop like a broken record. The room felt smaller, the silence thick and suffocating, settling between them like an unspoken barrier that couldn't be broken.

Donni reached for a bottle of water on the bedside table, his movements slow and measured. He poured a glass and handed it to Tasya, his voice low but steady. "Drink up," he said, the words laced with a quiet authority. "Yo, relax."

Tasya took the glass with both hands, her fingers trembling ever so slightly as she brought it to her lips. She sipped, the coolness of the water washing over her, and for a brief moment, she felt a strange, unexpected relief—as if the weight in her chest had eased just a little.

"Why'd you even sign up for this flight?" Donni asked, his voice a mix of curiosity and frustration, as if he couldn't quite grasp why she was still here.

Tasya lowered her gaze, the glass in her lap feeling heavier than before. "My mom," she murmured, her voice barely a whisper, as if she were speaking more to herself than to him.

"Your mom?" Donni repeated, his tone hanging in the air, as if the words themselves were drawing something out of her.

"I need a ton of money for her treatment, sir," Tasya said, her eyes glued to the glass in her lap. "I don't know where else I can get hundreds of thousands of dollars." She paused, taking a shaky breath. "I've already sold our house, sold everything... but her treatment's still not finished. That's why I joined Sky Royale—the salary, the tips—they're the best I could find."

"And I was just about to make you do something," Donni said, his breath escaping in a heavy sigh. "You've got me feeling like the worst damn person on earth."

"I'm sorry, sir," Tasya whispered, the words barely escaping her lips, heavy with guilt and something else—something she couldn't quite name.

"You know what the VIPs on SR flights usually expect from the attendants, don't you?" Donni leaned in, his grip on her arms tightening just enough to make her breath catch. "You're so damn gullible, Tasya. Fine. Let's do it this way." He shook his head, a flicker of something dark passing over his face as he met her gaze. "Like I said, just go back to your station. I'll still hook you up with a generous tip. Don't worry about it, alright?"

Tasya didn't move, still sitting beside Donni, as if her body had forgotten how to obey her mind.

"Tasya, what is it you really want?"

"Sorry, sir," Tasya muttered, her fingers twisting the satin of her skirt, the fabric slipping through her trembling hands as if trying to escape. "I thought I was ready for this. Thought I could handle it, take on the risks, be an SR flight attendant. But... turns out, I'm not that strong."

"And what?" Donni asked, his voice sharp, the question hanging in the air like a challenge, daring her to say more.

Tasya shut her eyes, taking a slow, steady breath, as if bracing herself for something she couldn't quite face. With hesitant hands, she reached out, her fingers trembling, and gripped Donni's hand, the weight of the moment settling between them.

"Tasya, what's going on?"

"If it's with you, Donni, I think I can get through it."

Donni stared at her, his eyes searching, as if trying to decipher the meaning behind her words. "What do you mean by that?"

Tasya guided his fingers to her chest, pressing them firmly against her, a wordless plea etched in the trembling of her hands. The warmth of his touch seeped through the thin satin of her uniform, making her flinch—a slight, involuntary shudder, as if the contact was too much, too intense, like a flame grazing tender skin.

She slowly opened her eyes, her gaze steady and unwavering, as she asked softly, "Do you still want this, Donni?"

6.

The private jet glided through the night, sleek and silent, a blade parting the velvet fabric of the sky. Above, the stars hung indifferent, their cold light distant and aloof. Below, clouds unfurled like restless whispers of forgotten dreams. Outside, the night pressed hard and sharp, its icy grip a reminder of the void beyond the glass. But inside the cabin, the air was feverish—alive with a heat that blurred the edges of reality. On the bed, they faced each other, mouths entwined in a kiss that burned with an unspoken, insatiable longing.

Tasya closed her eyes, her breath catching as Donni's lips brushed against her neck, the warmth of his breath mingling with the soft graze of his nose. Her skin came alive beneath his touch, each point of contact sending a spark racing through her—a flicker of something raw and primal stirring deep within.

She tilted her head back, surrendering completely, her posture an unspoken offering—a silent invitation for him to take whatever he desired.

"Your scent... it's intoxicating," Donni murmured, his voice a hushed reverence as he pressed his nose into the curve of Tasya's neck. He inhaled deeply, as if trying to capture her very essence, drawing it into himself like a vital breath.

Her fresh scent, laced with the faint, earthy tang of sweat, enveloped him in a heady, intoxicating blend—perfect in a way that defied words. His hand glided over her arm, down her back, tracing the curves of her body through the taut satin of her uniform. Each touch was slow, deliberate, as though he were claiming ground already achingly familiar.

"You've got me feeling drunk on you, Tasya," Donni whispered, his voice low and rough, the heat of his words brushing against her skin.

Without warning, his teeth sank into her neck—a sharp, possessive bite that sent a shiver racing down her spine. His lips latched onto the tender spot, sucking with a hunger that made her breath hitch. His grip tightened as he pressed her back, the room seeming to close in around them, the walls shrinking like the jaws of a trap.

Tasya reclined on the edge of the bed, her body sinking into the soft sheets as Donni hovered over her, his lips ravaging her neck with an insatiable hunger. Each kiss was a bite, a mark of possession, as if he couldn't get enough—her skin, a mystery he was desperate to unravel, each touch deeper than the last.

"Donni..." Her voice was a breathless whisper, trembling with need, the sound barely escaping her lips.

Her voice cracked, a tremor threading through each word as she bit down hard on her lip, the taste of iron sharp and bitter, like blood lingering on her tongue. Her fingers clutched the fabric of Donni's shirt, digging into it as if it were the only thing anchoring her to reality. Each of his licks, each pull of his mouth against her skin, left dark, lingering marks on her neck—like shadows that might never fade, haunting her with their intensity.

"Donni..." Her voice broke, soft and desperate, as if his name alone could hold her together in the swirling intensity of the moment.

Her whisper barely broke the silence, soft yet thick with something darker—a warning, or perhaps a desperate, silent plea. Donni's name lingered between them, trembling in the air, caught in her throat like it was too dangerous to speak aloud. Tasya's sighs, so soft, so haunting, curled around him, pulling him deeper into the moment like a siren's call. They only intensified the waiting, making the ache for what he desired feel unbearable. His hand traced the curve of her waist, the satin of her uniform gliding beneath his touch, before slowly lifting it, as if unveiling something long hidden.

Donni lifted the blouse just enough to expose the delicate curve of her neck, the fabric pulling back to reveal a black ornamental bra—semi-transparent, almost fragile, with a tiny ribbon at the center, serving as a clasp. It clung to her like it was struggling to contain her softness, the tension making it seem as though it might give way at any moment. Donni's gaze locked onto her, his smile stretching slowly, as if something inside him had been waiting to break free. It wasn't a friendly smile—not really. It was the kind of smile that knew something she didn't, savoring every second of the unfolding moment.

"Why's that, sir?" Tasya asked, her voice trembling ever so slightly, a flush rising up her neck.

The words tumbled out, awkward and too soft, as if they didn't belong in the space between them. The heat flooding her cheeks made the silence stretch, heavy and suffocating. Was something wrong with her? There was a sense she couldn't quite place, something crawling just beneath her skin, making everything feel unsettling, out of sync.

"You sure about the size?" Donni asked, his voice low as his fingers traced the fabric of Tasya's outfit, adjusting it with a touch that felt almost too deliberate. "Seems a little tight, like it's digging in... could be uncomfortable."

With a flick of his finger, the clasp of her bra snapped open, the sound sharp in the stillness, like the crack of breaking glass. Instantly, Tasya's breasts spilled free, as if released from an invisible restraint. The dark circles of her nipples stood out starkly against her pale skin, a striking contrast in the dim light, like something too exposed, too vulnerable.

Tasya inhaled sharply as the cold air from the AC brushed against the sensitive tips of her breasts. Strangely, her face began to burn, the heat rising up her neck and spreading into her cheeks.

She could feel it—Donni's gaze, heavy and unblinking, taking in every inch of her exposed skin. Her heart pounded as a rush of embarrassment swept over her, realizing that he was captivated by what she had, by the parts of her she couldn't hide.

She lay on the bed, her hair spilling around her like a dark, tangled halo. Her body was tense, as if she were trying to melt into the sheets. Her eyes flickered nervously, avoiding his gaze, a flush creeping up her neck—shy, yet fragile, like something on the edge of breaking.

"Goddamn it," Donni muttered under his breath, the words thick with frustration as the tension inside him snapped. He couldn't hold back anymore—the urge surged through him like an unstoppable wave, wild and relentless.

Tasya gasped, the sound escaping before she could stop it, as Donni's hand found her with unexpected precision. His touch was slow, deliberate—fingers pressing against her skin with an almost too-soft, too-careful tenderness. He cupped her breast, massaging it with steady, rhythmic pressure, as though savoring every inch of her, each motion unhurried, as if it were something that couldn't be rushed.

A soft moan escaped her lips, a breathless, involuntary sound that seemed to echo through the stillness.

The sound slipped from her lips, soft yet piercing, a blend of surprise and something unnameable—a ripple of shock coursing through her body. From Donni's mouth came the wet, rhythmic sounds of sucking, deliberate and indulgent, each one echoing with an intensity that spoke of total absorption. He seemed entirely lost in the act, as though her body was a banquet he could not resist.

His teeth grazed her nipple, followed by a gentle bite that tightened into a firm pull. His mouth worked with relentless fervor, his tongue flicking over the sensitive peak and leaving a slick trail of saliva that cooled against her heated skin. The shiver that followed raced down her spine, unrelenting and electric.

Meanwhile, his other hand gripped her opposite breast, his fingers twisting the nipple with a blend of roughness and precision that left her gasping. Her heart hammered in her chest, each thud reverberating through her trembling frame. The weight of his touch overwhelmed her senses, each caress pulling her deeper into a state she couldn't define.

Within her, something began to stir—slowly, insistently—a heat building low and potent, spreading like a fire threatening to consume her whole.

"Oh, wow," Tasya moaned, her voice a soft, breathy murmur, barely audible yet heavy with need. "Harder, sir." She bit down on her lip, her teeth sinking into the tender flesh as she tried to temper the sharp ache radiating from her breast—a sensation hovering precariously between pain and an intoxicating whisper of pleasure.

The cool, unyielding press of his lips melted into her skin, softening the sharp edge of discomfort like a balm soothing a raw wound. His touch held an inexplicable relief, dissolving the tension wound tightly within her, as though he instinctively knew how to dismantle her defenses, unraveling her piece by piece.

Tasya closed her eyes, sinking into the bed with an air of surrender, her body yielding to Donni's unrelenting hunger. His mouth moved from one breast to the other, devouring her with a fervor that felt insatiable. His hands roamed her flesh with calculated care, massaging and kneading with firm, deliberate motions, as though exploring the fullness beneath his fingers. Each squeeze was strong, almost possessive, yet tempered with a strange gentleness that left her suspended between resistance and submission.

She wasn't sure why, but her hands moved instinctively, fingers gripping the edge of her satin blouse as if to peel it away, to shed the layers that suddenly felt too confining. Just as she began to lift it, Donni's hand came to rest gently over hers, stopping her motion with a soft yet deliberate touch.

Donni paused, his gaze lingering on her face, studying it for a moment longer than she anticipated—a face shadowed with exhaustion, stretched thin by something unspoken. "That uniform suits you," he murmured, his voice low, intimate, like a secret meant only for her. "The satin's smooth, luxurious—just like you are right now."

The words were soft, but beneath them lay an undercurrent—something unspoken, tethered to a deeper truth he couldn't quite release. Her smile emerged slowly, quietly, spreading across her face as if she understood exactly what he meant, even without him saying it outright. And in that moment, it all clicked.

Tasya finally understood why her uniform had been tailored just a little too tight, the fabric clinging to her as if guarding a secret meant only for this moment. "So, can I take off your shirt, then?" she asked, her voice steady yet edged with intent, as though the question had already been answered in the silent tension lingering between them.

"Go ahead, Anastasia," Donni said, his voice steady and calm, yet carrying an undertone that made the words linger in the air, heavier than they should have been.

It was as if he were waiting for her, silently daring her to take the step without a word. Tasya's hand moved almost involuntarily toward the collar of his shirt, her fingers trembling ever so slightly as they brushed the fabric, feeling the warmth of his skin just beneath.

One button at a time, Tasya undid Donni's shirt, the metallic clicks sharp in the stillness. With each tug, the fabric parted further, unveiling the warmth of his skin beneath, the air between them thickening with every inch she exposed. Donni's hands guided hers, helping her slip the shirt from his body. It came away with a soft rustle, leaving a fleeting silence before the air hummed with something unspoken.

Tasya held her breath, her eyes tracing the lines of Donni's bare chest, so close she could feel the heat radiating from him. His broad shoulders, the muscles of his chest still sharp and defined, and the flatness of his stomach—all of it felt sculpted from stone. His body wasn't as pristine as the one she'd seen on stage, always shirtless and carefree. But now, the rawness of it, the weathered look of a man who had lived, only made him seem more real, more grounded. More... masculine.

The bold, spicy scent of his cologne filled her senses, clinging to him like a second skin, as if it belonged to him entirely. Without quite understanding why, Tasya's hands moved, drawn by an unspoken force, across the solid, muscular contours of Donni's body. His shoulders were firm, his chest like stone beneath her fingers, and his stomach held a hardness that spoke of strength and endurance. Each touch sparked something in her, a deepening curiosity with every inch she explored.

Tasya bit her lip, the sensation of Donni Firman's body against hers sharp and unexpected. She hadn't prepared for it, hadn't imagined it would feel so real, so immediate—like the weight of him was pressing deep into her bones.

"Can I continue celebrating this special night?"

"Go ahead, Donni," Tasya said, a soft laugh escaping her lips, as if she couldn't resist the pull of the moment.

Donni pressed a gentle kiss to Tasya's lips, a soft touch that lingered in the air. It was enough to make her smile, a warmth spreading within her, slowly creeping in like a comforting presence she hadn't anticipated.

Tasya cupped Donni's cheek, her fingers trembling ever so slightly as she leaned in, meeting his kiss with a fire of her own—hotter, more urgent, alive with passion. The soft yellow light from the cabin's overhead fixture bathed them both, casting a glow that made everything feel warmer, more intimate. The quiet of the room enveloped them, transforming the space into something else entirely—a place where the lines between fan and idol blurred, and the air thickened with desire.

"Mmm... yeah..." she murmured, her voice laced with a shadowy undertone, heavy and smoldering.

Donni's lips moved with an insatiable hunger, claiming hers again and again, as if he could never get enough. Tasya's lips, her taste, were utterly intoxicating. Her breath came faster, shallow and uneven, as a raw heat coursed through her. Her smooth, pale skin flushed under the weight of his relentless kisses, each one leaving a slick, glistening mark. Faint impressions of his teeth lingered, welts forming like whispers of his desire. The hem of her short skirt had slipped up to her stomach, leaving her exposed and vulnerable, as the air around them grew heavier, thick with suffocating tension.

Tasya wore a matching set of black, semi-transparent panties and a delicately ornamented bra, a perfect complement to her alluring form. Donni's hand slipped beneath the delicate fabric, his middle finger exploring the warmth within her. Tasya's waist squirmed in a slow, involuntary rhythm, her thighs gripping his hand tightly as his fingers moved with deliberate lightness, brushing against her most sensitive places. His lips claimed hers in deep, lingering kisses, while his mouth trailed to her breasts, alternately sucking and teasing. His hands roamed her body, caressing and squeezing with a practiced tenderness, each touch sending ripples of sensation coursing through her. Every movement seemed to converge on that singular point, where his fingers pressed and massaged with exquisite precision, amplifying the intensity until her nerves hummed with raw, uncontainable energy.

"Donni..." she groaned, her voice raw and guttural, as if it had clawed its way up from a dark, hidden place within her. The tension inside her coiled tighter and tighter, a mounting storm she could barely contain.

She was on the edge, teetering between control and something far more primal. If he didn't stop—if he didn't stop—she felt like she might unravel completely. "That's enough, sir," she whispered, her words trembling with urgency and restraint.

Donni's smile curved slowly, almost predatorily, as if savoring the moment. He complied with her request, withdrawing his finger with deliberate, unhurried precision. His middle finger glistened, coated with her wetness, the sheen catching the dim light in a way that felt almost otherworldly.

"Does that feel good, Tay?" he asked, his voice low and teasing, carrying a hint of knowing confidence.

Tasya turned her face away, the motion weak and faltering, as if even that small effort was too much. Her breath came in sharp, uneven gasps, her parted lips trembling as each exhale escaped. Her chest rose and fell in a frantic rhythm, her breasts heaving with the effort. A deep flush spread across her cheeks, radiating heat that betrayed the storm inside her. She didn't speak, but her body told the story—an answer as clear as any words could be.

She remained frozen, unable to move or utter a sound, as Donni pulled her black panties down in one smooth motion. The delicate fabric glided over her thick, pale thighs, slid past her long legs, and caught momentarily at her ankles before slipping away completely.

She was completely exposed now—her skin, a slightly deeper shade, contrasting against the paler tones of her body. The thin, meticulously groomed line of hair stood out, unnaturally precise in its neatness. Instinctively, Tasya moved to close her legs, to shield herself, but Donni's hand darted out, firm and unyielding, halting her movement.

Donni stood at the edge of the bed, unmoving, his gaze fixed on what lay before him as if it had anchored him in place, frozen in a silent, unspoken trance.

Tasya lay on the rumpled bed, her hair spread out like a dark halo around her. She wore a blouse, unbuttoned just enough, and a short blue satin skirt that had ridden up, leaving her breasts and womanhood exposed to the flickering, dim light. The soft glow from the cabin's faint illumination bathed her skin, casting shadows that highlighted the gentle curves of her body. Her face, beautiful yet weary, gazed upward with an expression of resignation, as if the weight of everything had sunk deep into her bones.

She was breathtaking, like a rare, dangerous masterpiece—one capable of stirring something dark in anyone foolish enough to gaze too long. Tasya felt Donni's hungry gaze trace every inch of her, and it sent a shiver through her, a rush of heat flooding beneath her skin. Was she really that captivating? Could she truly make someone feel this way?

"Please... stop staring, sir. I'm so embarrassed." Her voice trembled, the words soft but heavy with a mix of vulnerability and shame.

"Why are you embarrassed?" Donni chuckled, his fingers curling around hers, holding her captive. "Honestly, you look damn beautiful like this."

"Alright." Tasya bit her lip, the words bitter on her tongue as they slipped out. "Here I am... all alone... just naked."

Donni smiled, a slow, predatory curve of his lips, as he unbuckled his belt. The sharp clink of metal cut through the quiet room, loud and jarring, as he pulled it free and let it drop to the floor with a thud that seemed to reverberate in the stillness.

Tasya held her breath, unable to look away as Donni unfastened his pants, revealing himself fully. Her eyes were drawn to his erection—a thick shaft with prominent veins coursing along its length. It was a sight that etched itself into her mind, a surreal moment she could scarcely believe. For a devoted fan of Donni Firman for ten years, this was something Tasya knew she would never forget: seeing her idol, bare and exposed, right before her.

Donni leaned in, his grin widening like a crack splintering across fragile glass, his eyes locking onto hers with an unnerving intensity. "What's the matter? Gonna keep staring, or are you gonna do something about it?" he teased, his voice a low drawl that sent a chill racing up her spine.

Tasya's heart raced as he approached, stopping just at the edge of the bed. His imposing frame loomed over her before he began to crawl forward, slow and deliberate. Her gaze remained fixed on the pendulous sway of his shaft, a visceral reminder of his presence, as his body closed the distance, enveloping her in its shadow.

"Oh my God, are you serious?" Tasya squeezed her eyes shut, as if shutting out the world could somehow dull the overwhelming intensity. The pressure was unbearable, her body taut and unyielding—every muscle clenched like a spring wound so tightly it felt ready to break.

Was this real? Could it truly be happening—she, Anastasia, and Donni Firman—naked in bed together? The very idea felt surreal, almost impossible. Yet here she was, on the verge of crossing a line she'd only ever dreamed about. She and Donni, intertwined in a way she could barely comprehend, intimate in ways that left her breathless. The chaotic storm of questions in her mind froze in an instant when she heard his voice—low, deep, and laced with a quiet danger—whispering in her ear.

"There's nothing to be scared of," Donni murmured, his breath warm and reassuring against her skin. "I've got you. I'm right here with you."

Tasya blinked her eyes open, and there he was—Donni's face so close she could feel the heat of his breath. One of his hands clasped both of her slender wrists in a firm, unyielding grip. Slowly, deliberately, he pushed her hands upward, pinning them above her head, leaving her completely at his mercy beneath him.

She lay motionless, frozen under Donni's piercing gaze, which seemed to strip away every layer of her, reaching straight into her soul. His dark brown eyes held her captive, their intensity rooting her in place, leaving her unable to move, completely ensnared by his grip.

"When I said tonight's gotta be celebrated, I meant it, Tasya," Donni murmured, his voice low and edged with a dark, intimate intensity. "Tonight's the night I met you—a woman who makes me feel something right here." He pressed closer, his breath warm and heavy with the lingering scent of whiskey, settling on her skin like a smothering veil. The aroma curled around her, thick and intoxicating, wrapping her in its smoky grasp.

His fingers grazed her cheek, barely a whisper of contact, before they trailed down her neck, slow and deliberate. They stopped at the tip of her nipple, where they lingered for a moment, a silent promise. Then, with a soft pinch, he sent a jolt through her, making her squirm in response.

"I'm damn lucky to be on this flight as a VIP," Donni murmured, his lips brushing beneath her arm as he inhaled the intoxicating sweetness of her perfume. The scent of her skin wrapped around him, a drug he couldn't resist.

Tasya felt Donni's tongue trace the sensitive skin of her armpit, hot and slippery. "Hahh..." A sharp, breathless gasp escaped her lips, followed by a slow, shaky exhale.

"Getting service like this from the most beautiful flight attendant... you, Tasya," Donni murmured, his words muffled as he bit and sucked at the side of her breast, the heat of his touch searing through her skin.

"Sir, that hurts," Tasya whimpered, her voice soft and fragile, the words barely escaping her lips.

"Aight, Anastasia, I've got a question for you," Donni murmured, his voice low and intimate. His hand guided himself, the head of his shaft brushing against Tasya's slick, swollen folds, glistening as it caught the warmth of her arousal. He lingered there, poised at the entrance of her womanhood, his gaze locking onto hers.

"Do you wanna make this night unforgettable?" he asked, his tone heavy with meaning, his eyes searching her face for an answer.

"Yeah, sir," Tasya gasped, her breath hitching in quick, uneven pulls. The pressure inside her swelled, relentless and impossible to ignore, her voice trembling as she surrendered. "I want to."

Donni sank his teeth softly into Tasya's neck, a sharp yet fleeting sensation that sent a shiver through her. Simultaneously, he eased his hips forward, guiding his shaft to slowly, deliberately penetrate her, the motion deliberate and intimate.

Tasya tilted her head back, her eyes tightly shut, lips parted in a silent gasp that never found its voice. Her back arched into a graceful bow, every nerve alight as she felt the unyielding thickness of Donni's shaft sliding into her with deliberate slowness. Inch by inch, he filled her, deeper and deeper, until he was fully immersed, pressing against the very edge of her limits. The sensation was overwhelming—a potent blend of fullness and pleasure that left her breathless.

Donni's lips curled into a sly grin, amusement flickering in his eyes as he took in Tasya's reaction. "Damn, Tasya," he murmured, his voice low and rich with admiration. "You're something else. Absolutely stunning."

8.

Panting heavily, Tasya struggled to catch her breath, each gasp sharp and ragged as Donni's hips moved rhythmically between her thighs. His thrusts were deliberate, filling her completely with every motion. She felt the undeniable weight of him pressing down—not just physically, but with an intensity that carried something deeper, something shadowed and unspoken."

Donni's voice was a low murmur, barely audible in the heavy, suffocating stillness. His mouth found her, and his tongue brushed lightly over her hardened nipple—a fleeting, electric touch that sent a shiver coursing through Tasya's body.

Tasya couldn't control her body—it writhed involuntarily, caught in a strange limbo where discomfort mingled with an unbearable heat, a sensation that burrowed beneath her skin and left her aching in ways she couldn't articulate. Her breath hitched, a sound escaping her lips as Donni's hands tightened around her, his fingers sinking into the softness of her buttocks with a force that sent a ripple of heat through her—unsettling yet undeniable.

The pressure made her inner walls tighten, amplifying every sensation as the tip of Donni's shaft pressed firmly against the deepest part of her. The faint hum of the jet engines outside was a distant backdrop, doing nothing to diminish the intensity that consumed them in this moment. With six hours left in their international flight, there was more than enough time to make the night even more unforgettable.

The wet, rhythmic sound of their connection filled the cabin with each thrust, Tasya's body responding instinctively to Donni's movements. His weight pressed heavily against her, grounding her as he hovered over her, his large frame enveloping her entirely.

Tasya couldn't deny the weight of his body pressing down on hers, a pressure that brought an unfamiliar comfort she couldn't quite grasp. His heavy, enveloping form surrounded her, offering a sense of security—like she was no longer lost in the world. The sound of her ragged, breathless gasps was a kind of music to Donni's ears, raw and intoxicating. Her breasts, firm and full, pressed against his hard chest, each movement sending ripples through her. The feeling of skin on skin, the delicate brush of her nipples against his, sent a shiver deep within her, making the moment feel more real, more intense than anything she had known before. There was no room left now—just the two of them, tangled together, erasing everything else.

She clung to him, her hands roaming over the contours of his body with a desperate urgency, as if trying to memorize every inch. She felt the taut muscles of his arm, the broad expanse of his back, which seemed to consume her, and the subtle shift of his waist—each movement igniting something deep within her, a fire she wasn't sure she wanted to extinguish. His body was like a map, and she traced its roads, its lines, the hidden paths she couldn't resist following.

"Tasya..." he murmured, his voice low and laden with something unspoken.

His voice sliced through the silence, a ragged sigh escaping him as his hips moved with slow, deliberate thrusts—like the inevitable tick of a clock counting down to something unavoidable. It wasn't rushed, but it was relentless, pressing forward with a force that was both gentle and impossible to ignore, each movement sinking deeper, harder, pushing them both to the edge.

"Hey," he said, his voice low, almost hesitant. "I'm really glad you're letting me in like this. Glad you're... sharing this with me."

"Same here," Tasya moaned, her grip tightening on Donni's body, as if she were afraid he'd slip away. "I'm so damn happy... because you're my VIP."

"Deadass," Donni murmured, his lips brushing softly against Tasya's cheek, then her forehead. Each kiss lingered just a little too long, as if he were marking her, claiming her in a quiet, intimate way.

"I can't even picture it," Tasya gasped, her breath coming in ragged bursts. "If tonight, my passenger wasn't you... I can't imagine it. If someone else had been in this position... it'd be a completely different vibe, you know?"

"Relax, that's enough," Donni murmured before pressing a firm kiss to Tasya's lips. "Not another word," he added, his voice low and commanding. He slid his hands to the back of her knees, lifting her legs effortlessly. Gently but firmly, he pushed them upward until her knees touched her shoulders, exposing her fully. Holding her securely in his arms, Donni bent her body into a position that left no space between them, his embrace both encompassing and unyielding.

Tasya's legs were spread so wide that it gave the man complete freedom to move, allowing him to thrust and press his hips with greater intensity. The tip of his penis pushed deeper, reaching the very limit of what Tasya could bear, each motion testing the boundaries of her endurance.

"Ugh... Sir..." Tasya moaned softly, her voice laced with indulgence as Donni's thick shaft stirred her deeply. "Hoo... Donni..." she murmured, biting her lip to suppress the overwhelming tide of emotions threatening to consume her.

This was what she had longed for, craved more deeply than she dared to admit. Each slow, deliberate movement sent ripples of pleasure coursing through her, their breaths falling into rhythm, bound by a hunger that felt raw and primal. Every touch, every shift carried an unspoken promise, a shared yearning that connected them in ways words could never capture. This wasn't just physical—it was something profound, something that made her feel complete. This was what making love was meant to be.

"Donni..." she whispered, her voice trembling with a mix of vulnerability and desire, the name slipping from her lips like a prayer.

"Yeah, Tasya," Donni muttered, his voice low and thick, as if the words were caught somewhere deep inside, reluctant to escape.

"Make it harder, sir," she whispered, her voice trembling, as if challenging him to cross an unspoken boundary. "Harder, sir."

Donni smiled at Tasya's request, pausing his movements as he withdrew. His shaft glistened, slick with a mixture of her fluids, a faint frothy sheen betraying the intimacy of their shared moment.

"Why did you pull it out, sir?" Tasya's voice trembled, laden with a torrent of emotions she couldn't fully grasp. She didn't want to acknowledge the turmoil within, but the words escaped nonetheless—raw, jagged, and impossible to hold back.

For a moment, Donni stood motionless, his gaze locked on Tasya's body, slumped before him like a discarded rag doll. The silence between them stretched, heavy and suffocating.

Without a word, Donni bent down, his fingers skimming the floor before he straightened, something small and sharp glinting in his grip. "You want it rough, Anastasia?" he murmured, his tone laced with a dark edge. He closed the distance between them, his voice dropping lower. "Alright."

Tasya didn't resist. She allowed him to turn her, her body heavy and unresponsive as he flipped her face down onto the bed. A soft groan escaped her lips—a sound unfamiliar, almost unrecognizable as her own. Donni grabbed her hands, pulling them behind her back with deliberate force. Her eyes widened, her heartbeat quickening, as she felt the cold leather of his belt tighten around her wrists, binding them with a firm precision. The restraint felt like a silent promise—one she wasn't sure she was ready to accept.

"Donni..." Tasya breathed, her voice trembling as the bindings bit into her skin. "What do you want from me?"

"Don't be scared, Tay," Donni said, his voice smooth and coaxing, though it carried an undercurrent that felt unsettling. "I'm not gonna hurt you."

"But still..."

The words faltered, fragmented, as if they couldn't fully take shape. A heavy pause filled the air, thick with uncertainty—the kind of silence that lingers, hinting that whatever comes next could change everything.

"Tasya," Donni murmured, his voice soft, almost tender, as he pressed a lingering kiss to her cheek. Without warning, he slipped his hands around her waist, pulling her closer. "Just listen to me," he whispered, his tone low and urgent. "Trust me, aight?"

Tasya kneeled at the edge of the bed, her hands securely bound behind her back. Her knees pressed into the mattress, subtly arching her posture. The cool, conditioned air brushed against her exposed skin, eliciting an involuntary shiver. Every detail of her form seemed amplified by the soft lighting in the room, casting a shadow that highlighted her vulnerability.

"Sir?" she whispered, her voice barely audible as her eyes clenched shut, a rush of warmth spreading across her cheeks.

Donni gripped the waistline of Tasya's satin skirt, guiding himself with deliberate intent toward her.

Tasya released a soft moan, her eyes fluttering closed as the sensation washed over her—a feeling that was different, more intense than before. She could feel Donni pressing deeper, each movement deliberate and consuming. When he fully buried himself, the depth sent a shiver through her, her body responding instinctively as he pressed firmly against her.

"Ain't it good, Tay?" Donni murmured, his voice a low, gravelly rasp, like the whisper of wind through the trees on a long-forgotten road.

Tasya nodded slowly, her movements deliberate, her eyes shadowed with an unreadable emotion. In all her twenty-three years, she had never experienced anything like this. Yet deep down, with a certainty that sent a shiver down her spine, she knew—this time, she might actually like it.

Donni gripped Tasya's waist, his movements slow and deliberate as his hips began to rock. He couldn't help but notice how tightly she enveloped him, their bodies moving in a seamless rhythm. The sight, the sensation—it was exhilarating, a tantalizing blend of excitement and desire that sent a thrill coursing through him.

"Do you want me to go harder? To turn up the intensity?"

Tasya nodded slowly, almost hesitantly, as though the gesture itself carried a weight she wasn't ready to bear.

Donni bit his lip, drawing in a sharp breath, the kind that burned with intensity. Then, with sudden urgency, he thrust his hips forward, the movement raw and driven.

9.

The sound of Tasya's hips meeting Donni's waist echoed sharply within the confines of the bedroom cabin, each impact resonating through the space like a drumbeat. The rhythmic creaking of the bed underscored his relentless movements, a symphony of intensity that filled the air. Tasya's hands, tied firmly behind her back, clenched into fists so tight her knuckles turned white, a physical manifestation of the overwhelming sensations coursing through her.

Each thrust was deliberate, powerful, and unyielding, the rapid friction igniting a fire deep within her. The thickness of him stretched and pressed in ways that left her gasping, her inner walls hot and trembling, the sensation almost too much to bear. Her heart pounded in her chest like a wild drum, a primal rhythm that matched the pace of his relentless advance.

It was raw, untamed, and unlike anything she'd ever experienced. Tasya's breath came in sharp, frantic bursts as pleasure surged through her with every movement, building to an uncontainable crescendo. Her body, consumed by the moment, surrendered completely to the wild intensity. It wasn't just the act itself—it was the way it unleashed something buried deep within her. She realized, with a mix of exhilaration and abandon, that she craved this unbridled, primal connection. Each thrust sent her closer to the edge, and all she wanted was to lose herself in the explosive, unrelenting pleasure.

Tasya bit down hard, her teeth pressing together with such force she feared they might draw blood. Desperation clawed at her as she buried her face into the bed sheets, the fabric muffling her sounds. She pressed deeper, as though trying to vanish into the softness, determined to stifle the noise and keep it hidden from the world.

"Why, Tasya?" Donni gasped, his voice rough and uneven, as though the very question might shatter him. His hands clung to her fragile, unyielding form, desperate to keep her from slipping away, from retreating beyond his grasp. "Why are you holding back like that?" he demanded, his tone laced with frustration, his words raw with a simmering need that refused to be ignored.

"Ugh... I don't..." Tasya muttered, her voice dull and lifeless, as if the words themselves were too burdensome to bear, drained of all meaning before they could fully form.

Her voice hitched, snagging in her throat like a fish stranded on dry land. The sensation was raw, almost unbearable, as though any attempt to speak might set her words ablaze, scorching her from the inside out.

"I'm scared they'll hear... Captain," Tasya whispered, her voice quivering, each word fragile, as if even the air itself might conspire to betray her, carrying her fear to the wrong ears.

"To hell with them," Donni said, a crooked smile tugging at his lips as his gaze lingered on Tasya, dissecting her like an open book. "Nobody's gonna care what happens in this cabin. This is an SR flight, Tasya—passengers can do whatever the hell they want with the attendants."

"But... sir... maybe later... I think..." Tasya stammered, her words faltering, as if she were grasping for a way out that she couldn't quite find.

Donni didn't wait for her to finish. In one swift, almost feral motion, his right hand seized a fistful of Tasya's backside, silencing her unspoken words as if they held no significance at all.

With deliberate precision, his thumb pressed against the tight opening, the taut skin yielding slightly under the rhythmic motion. Each deliberate circle traced the shadowed ridges, his movements slow and methodical. Tasya's breath hitched sharply, caught in her throat, before a cry escaped—a raw, desperate sound that sliced through the room like a crack of thunder.

Her body trembled, unable to contain the intensity of it all—the press of Donni's waist against her, the deep, unrelenting thrust of his shaft within her, and the teasing, almost hypnotic motion of his touch. It was overwhelming, a heady blend of sensation that blurred the edges of her reality. Tasya's moans pierced the cabin's silence, her voice trembling with unrestrained pleasure as the weight of the moment consumed her.

"Ah... Ah... Donni..." Tasya whispered, her voice raw and trembling, as if pulled from the deepest, most vulnerable part of her soul.

Donni stayed silent, his movements steady as he thrust into Tasya, each motion deliberate and unrelenting. From behind, she seemed utterly surrendered, her vulnerability laid bare before him. Her moans and gasps, soft yet intoxicating, resonated like a haunting melody, weaving their way into his thoughts. Tasya, the devoted fan and flight attendant, her body adorned in a blue satin uniform that clung to her like a sculptor's masterpiece, exuded a striking elegance—like a living, breathing marble statue.

Tasya yielded to the desires of the VIP passenger, her resistance dissolving like a leaf carried away by a relentless current. In that moment, her beauty was almost haunting—a fragile, ethereal allure that seemed to transcend the reality around her.

Donni felt a peculiar, almost unsettling satisfaction as Tasya attended to him with unwavering devotion. This wasn't just any flight—it was Sky Royale, where every moment seemed charged with an air of heightened expectation.

Tasya gasped, her body writhing in a futile attempt to escape the overwhelming sensations coursing through her. The belt pressed into her skin, cold and unyielding, anchoring her firmly in Donni's grasp. Her dampened womanhood, slick with arousal, allowed his thick shaft to glide effortlessly, each movement stirring her depths with an almost maddening intensity.

"I don't know if I could bear it," Donni muttered, his voice low and rough, as he pressed his thumb firmly against Tasya. "The thought of some stranger touching you—feeling you, savoring every inch of you... It twists something inside me. You're my loyal fan, Tasya. Mine."

"Ugh... ughh..." Tasya moaned, her eyes tightly shut, as if trying to shut out a force she couldn't escape, something that refused to release its hold on her.

Her mind was a void, a dark and hollow expanse where everything else ceased to exist—everything but a single, throbbing point deep within her. It pulsed relentlessly, an unyielding rhythm that seemed to grow sharper with every beat, as though some unseen force was twisting it, driving it deeper into her very core.

"You're not serving anyone else but me on the next flight. You're mine, Tasya—my flight attendant," Donni growled, his grip tightening on the satin fabric of her skirt. His movements quickened, each thrust deliberate and forceful, driving the thick length of him deeper with unrelenting intensity.

Tasya couldn't summon the words to answer Donni; her mind felt like it had shut down, leaving her adrift in a hollow void. Her body moved, but it wasn't her—it was as if some detached force had taken over, guiding her motions without her consent. All she could register was the relentless, violent rhythm of his movements—a rhythm that seemed distant, disconnected from her. It was as though she were floating above it all, an unwilling observer to her own reality.

"Ughh... Haaaah..." The sounds escaped her lips in breathless, ragged gasps, heavy with unspoken emotion.

"You're mine," Donni rasped, his voice raw and jagged, each word cutting through the air like a blade etched with possession.

"Haaaah... Donni..." His name slipped from her lips, a trembling whisper laced with breathless intensity.

Her voice was scarcely more than a whisper, a breathless exhale as her half-closed eyes fluttered. Her gaze flickered through the tangled strands of her long hair, clinging to her face like remnants of her unraveling torment.

"That's enough, sir... please, enough..." Her voice wavered, a fragile plea barely holding back the weight of her trembling resolve.

"Yo... why, Tasya...?" Donni gasped, his breath ragged and uneven, each word strained as if he were grappling for air in a room that seemed to collapse around him.

"That's enough, sir... for real..." Tasya's voice trembled, the words laced with unease as a chilling sensation crept through her, like cold fingers trailing across her skin.

Just a little longer. A little more. The storm inside her coiled tighter, threatening to tear her apart. She could feel it—teetering on the edge, ready to snap, to shatter the fragile seams of her control.

"I can't deal with this..." Tasya muttered, the words scraping from her throat as if they were desperately trying to break free.

Donni could feel it too—the warmth within Tasya growing, a soft, sultry heat enveloping him. Her walls tightened, their embrace firm and pulsing, as if inviting him deeper. The sensation was intoxicating, a perfect blend of pressure and pleasure that made his breath hitch.

Tasya's breath hitched, her voice trembling in a barely audible whisper. "Sir...?" she gasped, each word laced with the weight of Donni's intensifying movements.

Donni's thrusts grew harder, faster, each one more relentless than the last—a rhythm of raw urgency, like an unyielding tide crashing against her. Tasya's skin tingled and burned where his hands gripped her, her buttocks and inner thighs flushed and tender from the sheer intensity of his movements.

"Donni..." she breathed, his name slipping from her lips like a plea, heavy with unspoken emotion.

The word escaped her lips, scarcely more than a breath, as she hovered on the brink. Every nerve in her body urged release, yet she had already surrendered—there was no retreat from the precipice she'd crossed.

Tasya didn't want to leave her mark on him, didn't want to scar the man behind her with something irrevocable. She battled fiercely to contain the storm surging within her, her voice quivering as she managed a trembling whisper: "Enough, sir..."

Instead of retreating, something inside her coiled tighter, like a vise locking into place. The tension seemed to ignite something primal in Donni, driving him to push harder, his movements growing more forceful, almost savage, as if the tightening walls within her were challenging him to go deeper, to claim more.

Donni sensed it in the air—the taut tension in her body, the unsteady catch in her breath. He knew with certainty that Tasya was on the brink, teetering at the edge of control, poised to cross the point of no return.

"Sir... I—I..."

Tasya's words fractured, her body twisting beneath him as her teeth sank into her lip, fighting to swallow something dark, something she couldn't confront. Yet that darkness clawed its way up, relentlessly pushing its way to the surface. Her hand tightened into a fist, the pain so fierce it felt as if her bones might splinter.

"Aah... Nngh..."

With a decisive motion, Donni freed Tasya from the tension that had gripped her. As he withdrew, a rush of clear liquid cascaded from her, flowing freely—a release as overwhelming as it was uncontrollable. It surged like a torrent, soaking the pristine white sheets and pooling on the cabin floor, a tempest of emotions made tangible. In that moment, Tasya felt untethered, soaring high without wings, suspended in the euphoria of her own sensations. Her moan erupted into the room, raw and unrestrained, a visceral sound that seemed to rise from the deepest parts of her being, reverberating like the cry of a soul laid bare.

Tasya crumpled onto the bed, her body limp and spent, the belt biting sharply into her wrists, bound tightly behind her—a stark reminder of the intensity she had just endured. Her legs trembled, spasms coursing through her in uneven waves, her body jerking involuntarily as the remnants of pleasure pulsed through her, refusing to fade completely.

Donni stood a few feet away, his skin glistening with sweat, each drop a marker of the raw energy he'd poured into the moment. Every ounce of effort had been worth it. Before him, the flight attendant lay crumpled on the bed, her body trembling, the satin of her uniform disheveled and creased from the frenzied passion that had unfolded. It was an unforgettable sight—a haunting blend of beauty and chaos, like a vivid fragment of a fever dream brought to life under the dim glow of an eighteen-hour flight.

He exhaled deeply, a slow smile spreading across his face—the kind that comes when you know you've stepped beyond an unseen boundary. His body still thrummed with the afterglow, a deep, resonant pulse centered where the memory of her warmth lingered. It was an unshakable connection, hanging in the air like a shadow, intimate and undeniable.

He teetered on the edge, dangerously close to the brink. Donni sank into the chair, utterly spent, his chest heaving with ragged breaths. Reaching for a bottle of mineral water from the minibar, he twisted off the cap and drank deeply, the icy liquid surging through him, quenching the fire still smoldering within.

Tasya lay motionless on the bed, her hair falling in tangled waves, a dark curtain concealing her face like a shadowed secret. Her shoulders rose and fell with sharp, uneven breaths, each gasp fighting against the weight of the thick, stifling air around her.

She couldn't move, her body heavy and unyielding, every muscle crying out in utter exhaustion. Even opening her eyes felt insurmountable, as if the effort might shatter her entirely. All she could do was remain still, her head spinning in a slow, disorienting spiral, the edges of the room fading into a hazy blur.

She craved rest—desperately. For several long minutes, the cabin was steeped in silence, thick and oppressive, as if the air itself held its breath, trapping the echoes of a moment too raw, too intense to dissipate. This flight would be etched in memory, for both the passenger and the flight attendant.

"Tasya." Donni rose from the chair, his movements unhurried, deliberate, as though the weight of the moment pressed heavily upon him. He crossed the room toward her, his voice low and subdued, barely more than a murmur. "Are you finished?"

"Yeah, sir," Tasya mumbled, her voice barely a whisper, swallowed by the heavy fog of exhaustion that clung to her like a second skin.

Donni ran a hand through his hair, his brow furrowed in faint confusion. "Thing is," he murmured, his voice low, almost to himself, "I haven't." A dark chuckle escaped him, tinged with something unsettling. "Still rock hard, can you believe that?" Without waiting for a response, he grabbed Tasya's thighs with a firm, almost possessive grip, rolling her onto her back against the damp, clinging sheets.

"Wait, sir," Tasya whispered, her voice trembling and frail, the protest fading before it fully formed. "I'm still..." Her words faltered, swallowed by exhaustion and resignation. Powerless, she could only surrender as Donni positioned himself, the head of his erection pressing against her slick, tender entrance, the moment fraught with an unspoken intensity.

With measured force, Donni thrust his rigid length back into Tasya, the movement charged with unyielding intensity.

A guttural "Ughhh!" escaped her, raw and primal, cutting through the silence like a visceral release.

10.

The night remained a vast canvas of darkness, punctuated by faint starlight, as the private jet descended toward Bangkok's runway. The tarmac lights glowed softly, less a guide and more a conspiratorial wink, welcoming the aircraft back from its grueling eighteen-hour journey. The wheels met the asphalt with a subdued screech—an understated punctuation to the voyage. Flaps unfolded like weary wings, slowing the jet with graceful precision as it coasted off the main strip, its nose turning toward a private hangar. The airline's insignia stood tall on the tail fin, a proud declaration against the night sky.

Waiting ahead was a sleek black car, more than mere transportation—a symbol of privilege, an unspoken promise of exclusivity. This wasn't just any flight; this was Sky Royale. Yet as the minutes stretched and the fuselage remained sealed, the air grew thick with curiosity. The VIP passenger hadn't stepped out. Not yet.

He fastened the final button of his shirt, his movements slow and deliberate, as if savoring the ritual. His gaze swept over the cabin bedroom—a tableau of controlled chaos steeped in sweat, wine, and something raw, almost feral. The bed was a skewed mess, shoved slightly off-center, its sheet pulled free and tangled like a creature caught mid-escape. Damp wrinkles stretched across the fabric, silent witnesses to Tasya's restless energy. Empty wine bottles leaned precariously on the table, surrounded by scattered remnants of the night.

Donni's lips curved into a self-satisfied smile. It wasn't tidy, it wasn't polished—but it was perfect in its disarray.

Tasya stood near the door, fingers deftly twisting her hair into a hasty bun—a rushed, almost desperate attempt to tidy herself, as if trying to erase the remnants of something she couldn't quite forget. Her blue satin uniform clung to her body, wrinkled and damp in places, bearing the unmistakable marks of a day that had been far from ordinary. When she turned, their eyes met, locking for a fleeting moment.

In that instant, she felt herself slipping back, caught in the memory of the flight—the stolen moments, each one a quiet, forbidden indulgence that lingered just beneath her skin.

Donni had been relentless, driven by a hunger that felt insatiable, as though only she held the key to what he so desperately craved.

And Tasya had yielded.

Again and again, Donni had gifted her experiences that would etch themselves into her mind—moments she'd never be able to forget. And Tasya?

Tasya had absorbed it all, each moment, as if starving for it—every touch a feast. She could still feel the burn of his hands, the weight of his body pressed against hers, his lips mapping her skin, leaving trails of fire in their wake. Even now, she could recall the fullness of him, the tightness, the way he'd filled her, marking her in a way that would never fade. Her face flushed deep red, the heat rising once more. It felt unreal, like a dream—too vivid, too sharp, too real to be anything but tangible.

"All done with the touch-up?" Donni asked, his voice low, almost a whisper. He moved toward her with slow, deliberate steps, as if savoring every moment.

"Is it still showing, sir?" Tasya asked, her voice trembling just enough to make you question whether she truly wanted the answer. She fidgeted with the hem of her short skirt, tugging at it as if she could somehow make it fall lower, hide what she couldn't quite erase.

"So what if it does?" Donni teased, a wicked grin spreading across his face, as if he knew exactly how to twist the knife.

"I'm so embarrassed in front of the captains," Tasya pouted, her voice laced with a blend of frustration and something more—like she was masking a darker, deeper emotion behind that pout.

Donni slipped his arm around her waist, his fingers grazing the soft, defined curves hidden beneath her tight uniform. "No need to be embarrassed," he murmured, his voice smooth and low. "You gave your passenger the best service."

He turned her toward him, his hands guiding her gently until her shoulders met the cold, unyielding door of the cabin. Then, with quiet intensity, he claimed her lips again, marking her in the silence that followed, as if she were his and his alone.

"Mmhh..." Tasya gripped his muscular arms, her pulse racing in her chest, savoring the farewell kiss as if it were the last taste of something forbidden—the kind of kiss that lingered long after the flight had ended, impossible to forget.

"What's up?" Donni asked, pulling back just enough to study her face. He wiped the tear from her cheek with his thumb, the gesture surprisingly gentle, as if he understood something she wasn't ready to voice.

"After this, then," Tasya said, her words hanging in the air, thick with something she couldn't quite name—perhaps a promise, perhaps a warning, though it was hard to tell which. She half-sobbed, her fingers trembling as they nervously played with his shirt collar. "Are you going to forget about me, Donni?"

"Huh?" Donni muttered, his voice low and heavy, as if he were struggling to make sense of something just beyond his grasp.

"Once this is over, you'll just slip back into your busy life, right? Back to being the famous singer," Tasya said, her voice tight, her teeth biting down on her lip. "Am I just going to fade away for you?"

Donni kissed her again, a deep, burning kiss that lingered, holding onto the moment as if trying to freeze time. "How could I forget this, Tasya?" he whispered, his lips so close that each word grazed hers. "You make me want you so damn bad. Everything about you screams that I need you, that you should be mine."

He slipped his hand beneath her satin skirt, reaching for the intimacy they both understood too well. His fingers found a spot, pressed gently, and massaged it, sending a rush of weakness through her legs—like she might collapse if he let go.

"Donni..." Tasya tilted her head back, her mouth slightly open, as if she were on the verge of saying something but couldn't quite find the words.

"I can't stand the thought of anyone else touching this. It's mine, isn't it, Tasya?" Donni asked, his voice low and raw, as if the words were ripping out of him.

Tasya nodded, her head jerking slightly, as if the motion was the only thing anchoring her in the moment.

She stepped out first, her feet dragging slightly, the weight of her duty as a flight attendant still pressing down on her. Her job wasn't over until the VIP passenger was safely off the plane.

She staggered toward the exit, her movements almost mechanical, as if something had broken inside her. The captain and co-pilot stood by the cockpit door, watching her with eyes that were too sharp, too knowing. As she passed the captain, her face flushed a deep red, her head dropping to avoid his gaze. But his smirk lingered, cold and knowing, like a mark she couldn't erase.

She reached for the door, her hand trembling slightly, and opened it for the VIP. Behind her, the captain removed his hat and extended his hand to Donni, the gesture deliberate, almost too polite, as if something unspoken hung between them in the heavy silence.

"Thanks for flying with us," the captain said, her voice a bit too sweet, like someone who'd delivered the line a thousand times. "How did you find our SR service, sir?"

Donni gave a quick, almost dismissive nod, his gaze flickering briefly to Tasya before returning to the captain. "In a week," he said, his voice steady but carrying an edge beneath the calm, "I'll be flying back to New York. I want Tasya handling my SR flight."

His words dropped into the silence like stones sinking into deep water, something unspoken swirling just beneath the surface. The captain's eyes flicked to Tasya, a quick, knowing wink followed by a thumbs-up—casual, yet heavy with unspoken meaning.

"Tasya took real good care of you, didn't she, sir?"

"The best, hands down," Donni replied, his words smooth as oil. He pressed a quick, almost careless kiss to Tasya's lips, a fleeting touch that left something lingering, then turned and descended the aircraft steps, his back rigid, as if he couldn't escape fast enough.

Tasya stood there, frozen, her eyes following Donni as he slid into the waiting car. She didn't move, not even when the car eased away, leaving the hangar—and her—behind. The hum of the engine faded, swallowed by the stillness. Then, like a jolt of electricity, her phone buzzed, the sound slicing through the quiet with a sharp, urgent sting.

She picked up the phone, her fingers trembling as she unlocked it. When the message from Donni appeared on the screen, her breath hitched. Her eyes widened, unable to tear herself away from the number—far more than she'd expected. *Hope this helps with your mother's treatment,* the message read, simple, almost unnervingly cold for something so heavy.

Don't miss out!

Visit the website below and you can sign up to receive emails whenever Frank Spreader publishes a new book. There's no charge and no obligation.

https://books2read.com/r/B-A-QABKB-OPXKF

Did you love *Sky Royale: A Flight of Desire and Dissonance*? Then you should read *Shadows of Skull Valley*[1] by Frank Spreader!

[2]

In the heart of Backbone Mountain, a deadly storm brews as four mysterious maidens in skull masks rise from a forgotten valley, heralding the birth of the sinister Skull Valley Clan. As they wreak havoc across the martial world, the legendary Sword Deity of Kentucke Country establishes the Sweet Lake Sect in a desperate bid for peace. But when the enigmatic Dragon Fire Axe Warrior, Wintie Rayado, crosses paths with the deadly Green Scorpion, the stage is set for a brutal clash of power, revenge, and forbidden passion. As the twelfth day of the twelfth month approaches, the martial world trembles, and the fates of heroes and villains alike hang in the balance. *Shadows of Skull Valley* is an epic

1. https://books2read.com/u/mK8aY5

2. https://books2read.com/u/mK8aY5

tale of deadly ambition, ruthless martial prowess, and a love that defies even the darkest of destinies.

Also by Frank Spreader

The Dragon Warrior

The Vengeance of the Mighty

Echoes of the Cuchillo

Shadows of Skull Valley

A Wedding to Die For

Standalone

Fond Memory in Indian Rocks Beach

Piece of Life: Undeserved Maid

Piece of Life: Adolescent Adventure

Piece of Life: Dramatic Karma

Piece of Life: Back to Hometown pt. 1

Piece of Life: Back to Hometown pt. 2

Piece of Life: Hillary, a Desperate Housewife

Lover's Smile pt. 1

Lover's Smile pt. 2

Lover's Smile pt. 3

Lover's Smile pt. 4

Dark Secrets

Dark Secrets II: A Long Sweet Night

Dark Secrets III: Too Fast to Die

Dark Secrets IV: Lost in the Echo

Dark Secrets V: One Step Closer
Dark Secrets VI: High Voltage
Revenge
Revenge II: Final Masquerade
Revenge: The Little Things You Give Me Away
Dark Lantern
Lily: The Story of a Call Girl, Part One
Lily: The Story of a Call Girl, Part Two
Lily: The Story of a Call Girl, Part Three
Lily Loves This Game
The Challenge for Lily
Lily Exceeds the Limit
The Bed Is Stained
Old Man & a Virgin
Jennifer's Nuptials
Dakota
Abused Billie: Part One
Abused Billie: Part Two
Rise of the Pervert
Jesslyn's Tragedy
Fall of the Pride
Home Alone
My Beloved Lecturer
Sex after Lunch
The Illicit Conspiracy
The Waiting Time
Quartet of Whiskers from the Abyss Within
Entangled Deceit: A Reflection on Second Chances
Echoes of Mortal Melodies in the New Realm of León
Echoes of Deceit: A Tapestry of Broken Hearts
The Stranger at Home
Sky Royale: A Flight of Desire and Dissonance

About the Author

Frank Spreader is a passionate storyteller who weaves tales that explore the complexities of human relationships, desire, and ambition. With a deep appreciation for the intricacies of interpersonal dynamics, Frank creates characters who are as flawed and vulnerable as they are compelling.

Drawing inspiration from the worlds of luxury, fame, and the hidden struggles beneath polished surfaces, Frank delves into the delicate balance between aspiration and authenticity. When not writing, Frank enjoys traveling, indulging in music that stirs the soul, and finding beauty in the ordinary.

This story is a testament to Frank's fascination with moments that define us—the choices we make when faced with temptation and the courage it takes to hold onto our values.

www.ingramcontent.com/pod-product-compliance
Lightning Source LLC
LaVergne TN
LVHW090126160826
845673LV00015B/1026
9798230321484